Reflections
By Lynn Rosen

Introduction

In this book Rocket Man & Poetry Lady face many hardships. Poetry tries to help him but he totally ignores her. She decides to give him a taste of his own medicine.

This book will keep you on the edge of your seat.

Dedication

I dedicate this book to the man who made my heart smile. Thank you for showing me that no matter how tough life is, it will get better. You are the best husband in this world.

Chapter One
Heartache

Rocket Man was not feeling well. Poetry told him she thought he had the flu. She took him to the doctor and he agreed with Poetry. She loved when he agreed with her. His fever was very high and he kept trying to sleep.

The doctor decided to let him spend a day or two in the hospital. He had small children and he would be more comfortable there.

Poetry came there after she took the kids to school. He was so pale. To her it didn't look like he was getting better. His fever broke on the weekend and he was finally released. He was so happy at that moment.

What struck Rocket as strange was that his mother never came to the hospital. Poetry told him that she couldn't reach his mother. She was nowhere to be seen. Now Rocket was concerned. He started calling and finally she answered. She was okay. She just was very busy. Poetry was a mother too. She would never be too busy for her children.

After Poetry got Rocket settled in she went to see his mother. She needed to understand why his mother didn't visit him. For all intents and purposes.

When she got to her home she rang the bell. There was no answer. Where was his mother? She showed up an hour later. She told them that she was busy spending time with her friend. She also told Poetry that she had her own life. She was sick of babysitting.

Poetry walked out. She was disgusted with her.
She got home in time to make Rocket dinner.

Chapter Two
Gone and Forgotten

Rocket was quite upset. His own mother didn't care if he was alive or dead. Men were more important than her son. He was depressed. He was healing but sadness was his mantra. Poetry doted over him. She loved him.

She told him that soon they would be back to work. He said that he didn't care. She hired a nurse to take care of him. He was so weak and she still had the kids to take care of.

Louella Larsen was a nurse since she hit the age of 30. She loved taking care of others. When she saw Rocket's depression she told him that he should be ashamed of himself. He had a beautiful family, a house that was in the best part of California and food on his table. It took a full month for the flu to leave Rocket's body. When it did he seemed back to his old self. He was ready to go back to work. He hated saying goodbye to Louella but he did anyway.

He spent the weekend with Poetry and the kids and he felt so lucky to be alive. It was a Sunday morning and they decided to go out to breakfast. The doorbell rang. Rocket went to answer it. It was his mother.

She was carrying several bags. She went to hug him
and he moved away. Why would he hug a woman who
didn't care enough to come to see him when he needed
her and instead was playing around with men.... He
told her that she was gone from his life. He didn't need
her and neither did his family. Tears streamed down
his face. He then started to close the door but Ryan
heard his grandma's voice. He was excited. He ran out
to hug her and invited her to breakfast with them. She
came in. In the bags were gifts for the kids and for
Rocket Man & Poetry Lady.

After opening the gifts, they went to breakfast. Rocket Man's mother drove in a car with Poetry Lady. Rocket drove with his kids.

They arrived at the Pancake House. They knew it would be crowded but they could wait. They were in no rush.

The kids insisted that grandma sit between them. What Poetry found interesting is that they never even asked her where she had been. In the car they had discussed small talk but now she just was enjoying her grandchildren.

Food came out on trays. They had pancakes, French toast and lots of bacon. Rocket Man had eggs with his pancakes and sausage. The kids wanted malted and Rocket never could say no to them.

When breakfast was over Poetry took the children home in her car. She was hoping that Rocket could get a chance to talk to his mom.

On the way home his mom sat there and he didn't say a word. Finally, she started to cry. He asked her why she was acting like she cared and she responded by saying she did care and she would tell him why she hadn't seen him while he was sick.

As she told her story his face turned red. He called Poetry and told her to leave the kids at her mother's and meet him at Starbucks. He told her that it was urgent.

When Poetry Lady got to Starbucks she pulled next to Rocket's car. She loved Starbucks and was there every single day.

She was surprised to see Rocket holding his mother's hand but happy at the same time. In a few minutes Dave appeared. Then Rocket Man's mother told her story. Poetry Lady felt sick.

Rocket looked so angry.

She began," A few days before Rocket got sick an old friend visited me. He was a lawyer and he was a good friend when she needed one. They were not involved at all. He showed her a picture that would change her life forever. It was a picture of his father. Thus the adventure began. "

Rocket Man's father died several years ago of cancer. Robert, a mutual friend of both of theirs claimed that he saw him in New York. She insisted he was dead.

That is why she disappeared. She was searching for his father. Although they were divorced she had a strange feeling that he could be alive. He hadn't been cremated so anything was possible. He was staying right near Central Park.

She went to the apartment where he was spotted in Central Park West. She showed his picture to the doorman. He knew him and told her that he just left. He was on his way to see a Broadway show.

He was seeing Phantom of the Opera. She then went to the theater with her friend to see if he was there. To her surprise he was quite alive.

When he saw her he turned red. Then he left the theater with her while his lady friend saw Phantom.

Chapter Three
A Tale of Woe

Rocket knew he had to find his father. He grieved for him for so long. He had to tell him what he thought of him. His mother told him where he was. He looked at Poetry Lady. She understood that he had to fly to New York.

He took a taxi to the hotel where his father was staying. His father had been expecting him. Rocket got an opportunity to release the angst he felt inside. His father explained that at the time that he disappeared he was sure he was dying. He did this for his family. Rocket Man called him a coward.

Both Rocket and his father flew home on the next day. When Poetry saw his father she was just so glad that he was alive. Rocket glared at him. The children were confused but they ran into his arms.

Rocket's father was home for good. He knew he had to mend fences and this could take some time. He just wouldn't give up until he accomplished what he set out to. Rocket's mother showed compassion for her son. She knew how he must feel.

Poetry was proud of the way that Rocket handled this.

Chapter Four

Evening The Score

Rocket was good at hiding his feelings. Poetry knew that better than anyone. She nevertheless had compassion for him. To find out that your father lied to you was difficult.

Poetry had an idea. She invited Rocket out to dinner but he said he would rather stay home. She had an idea. She got tickets for his favorite basketball team. They went to watch the game. He loved the game and after the game they went to dinner. It was a night to remember because Rocket's team won.

The next week his father tried to contact him but he ignored the calls. Rocket told Poetry that he had no intention of talking to his father. Poetry told him that he might regret it one day and he ignored her.

It was a Friday night and the telephone was ringing.
She answered and it was Rocket's mother. She needed
to speak to her son. Poetry said that he wasn't taking
calls.

On Saturday he took the kids to the park. There were
rides and they were having a ball. Then he saw his
father. His father approached the kids. He told Rocket
Man that they were his grandchildren and he had a
right to see them. At that very moment he put the kids
in the car and took off.

Chapter Five
A Day in Court

Rocket Man was shocked when he was served legal
papers. His father was suing him for not allowing him
to see the kids. He had been angry one day. What kind
of father does something like this?

Poetry tried to talk to him but he refused to give in. Rocket glared at his father. When the judge ordered him to let his father see his grandchildren Rocket Man was fuming. His mother took his hand. Poetry was angry with him. They could have compromised but that wasn't a word that Rocket knew.

Rocket told the entire story to the judge and when the judge rendered his decision Rocket said he wouldn't do this. The judge said he had to. Finally, the judge told the bailiff to take him to jail.

For two weeks he sat in prison. Poetry came to visit him. She told him to stop being so angry and understand that everyone made mistakes. After she left he thought of everything she said. Finally, he asked to see the judge.

Poetry went to the jail to pick him up. He wasn't there.
He left early that morning. She went to the office and
to his father's apartment. He was nowhere to be found.

Chapter Six
Peace

Poetry Lady was concerned about Rocket Man. No
matter how crazy he got he always talked to her. She
stayed at the office because she could concentrate
more. She called Dave and he told her he hadn't
spoken to Rocket in a few days.

When the phone rang she was relieved. It was Rocket.
He was sitting in their favorite spot looking at the
mountains and inhaling. He was taking deep breaths as
she taught him to do. She told him that she would be
there soon.

When she pulled up to the spot he was standing and
looking at the water. She smiled at him and he melted
when he saw that smile.

He told her that he arranged to speak to his father. They were going for coffee in an hour. He just needed peace and as they stood there they knew they were at the right place.

Rocket left to speak to his father and Poetry went home. She knew that they had to be alone. She headed for the shopping mall. She needed to buy clothing for the children.

When she got home Rocket Man was waiting for her.
He told her everything was great with his father now.
They had made peace. She showed him the clothing
she bought and he asked her if she left anything for
others to buy. She laughed and she went to put the
clothing away.

When she returned to the room Rocket was on the
phone and smiling. It was the children's school. Ryan
had been chosen as valedictorian. Both childen were
intelligent . He was so proud and so was she.

Rocket went to pick up the kids. When he told Ryan
how excited he was Ryan said it was nothing. He just
shook his head. They went home.

Chapter Seven
Poetry Plans

Poetry had to plan a graduation party for her kids. She
wanted it to be amazing. She would invite all of their
friends and family too.

She went to look at places. One place looked bigger
than the next.

She loved two venues and she asked Rocket Man to choose. He wanted it to be in good taste.

Poetry wanted the party at home and Rocket wanted a hall where the mess was there's.

After a week of searching they found the perfect place. They booked it and moved on the items that they needed.

With every passing day Poetry go more involved and she knew it would be a success. She compromised and chose the hall. It was a beautiful hall.

Ryan was the graduate but his sister would graduate the following year. She also helped in preparing for the party.

Rocket hired a DJ and they were good to go.

Chapter Eight
A Night to Remember

The night finally came. Poetry and Rocket dressed casually. Ryan looked so handsome. He was wearing a tuxedo. Their daughter wore a pretty taffeta dress. There were fifty friends and students invited. Ryan was very popular. He didn't realize just how wonderful he was but Poetry knew he would in time. She had watched her little boy grow up into a fine young man.

The party lasted four hours and Rocket Man was so glad when it was over. This was the first party to be held for the graduations. They still had their prom to attend and other parties given by parents. The night went off without a hitch. Poetry was so happy.

Driving home Ryan thanked them. Next year he would be off to college and she was sad about that but she knew that she had to let him spread his wings. They had visited many colleges but Ryan had a dream. He wanted to go to Columbia University. He loved New York.

His grades were fabulous and he aced the entrance exam. Poetry had a good friend in New York. If he got into trouble he could depend on her. He had a wonderful future ahead of him. Although they would miss him, they were very excited about his plans.

Chapter Nine
Graduation

Two weeks later graduation finally arrived. Since Ryan was valedictorian they got front row seats. Their daughter was in L.A. with her class. They had a special field trip. She didn't want to force her to go to graduation.

The lawn of the high school was where the graduation was taking place.

It was a long drawn out ceremony. She thought of how
handsome he looked before he attended the prom.
Now he was graduating. Poetry sat proudly listening to
speeches. Rocket Man kept yawning.

Finally, Ryan got up to give his speech. It was a
wonderful one. Everyone applauded when it was over.
Then came the moment when everyone tossed their
hats in the air.

Even Rocket had a smile on his face. After graduation
Rocket's parents and her parents joined them for lunch
at Ryan's favorite restaurant. He was now a college
man.

In a month he would be leaving for school and it would be an adjustment for him. He was never on his own. When they got home that night they sat and chatted with Ryan. He was so excited about school. Who wouldn't be?

He knew Poetry's friend only too well. They had visited her from time to time while growing up. Ryan had a thing about New York. It was a place where he eventually wanted to live. Now in a month he would be living there.

Chapter Ten
Getting Ready

For the next month or two Poetry Lady got ready for Ryan to leave the nest. She went shopping for new clothing for him. He hated trying on things but she explained that she couldn't buy things without him trying them on.

The month before he left for Columbia she had the booklist of everything he would need. She got all of the books and if they wanted additional reading he could get more at the Columbia University Book Store.

Rocket Man believed that Poetry was doing all of this not only to make it easier for Ryan but to keep busy so she didn't think of her loss. Rocket prepared him with lessons for life about drinking, staying out too late and told him that New York could be a dangerous place.

Regardless of how they would have liked to slow things down the time came for him to leave. His sister was busy with getting ready for school. This was her last year. Soon they would be empty nesters.

Poetry and Rocket accompanied Ryan for the first trip to Columbia. They wanted to drive cross country anyway and their daughter came too. The car was filled with clothing and items for his room. They bought crates and hangers and so much more.

When they finally got to Columbia they went into the dorm office to see where he was going to live. They had sent money but they had no clue as to where his dorm was. His dorm was right outside the school.

His roommate was already there. He had gotten there an hour before. Ryan had contacted him a month ago and they emailed and texted. They were like old friends. Rocket and Poetry stayed to help him unpack. When they said goodbye it was the toughest moment of their lives. What a loss this was but a great life lesson for Ryan.

They went to dinner with her friend. They were staying at their favorite Marriott for 2 nights. The Marriott Marquis was always their go to place when they were in New York.

Poetry was so happy to see her friend. Rocket went to the health club while Poetry and their daughter went shopping. He couldn't stand shopping with them. Poetry went from store to store. She never stopped. Poetry was heading for Lord & Taylor. They had great sales and one was going on right now.

They walked up and down Fifth Avenue. Finally, it was time to return to the hotel. They were both tired.

When they got to the hotel they were pleasantly surprised. Ryan was there with his roommate. He came to meet them for dinner. They had a wonderful dinner together and then went back to school.

The next day Poetry and Rocket let their daughter revisit the Museum of Natural History. It was one of her favorite places.

They then went to Central Park. After the park it was time for lunch. Rocket wanted to eat at Tavern on the Green. It was elegant and the food was fabulous. It was tough to get a reservation but he knew someone there. He had helped one of the waiters there.

They went home right after lunch. They had to get ready for their trip home. School started for their daughter in five days. Poetry had everything ready for her. That night they went to sleep early. The next morning, they left the hotel at eight. It would take a day or two to get home.

Chapter Eleven
Home Sweet Home

They were all happy to get home. Poetry called her parents to tell them she was home. Immediately her father wanted to see his granddaughter. Her mother was not at home when she called.

On Monday they went back to work. They had no open cases to work on but they knew that something would turn up. It always did. They were in the office for fifteen minutes when there was a knock at the door. It was Poetry's father. He needed to speak to them and home would not be a good place to do this. He was dating someone that he met recently. She was a sweet lady and there was lots of chemistry. Yet he felt there was something strange about her. She would see him for a few weeks and then she would say she was leaving town and disappear for a month at a time. He wanted them to investigate and find out exactly what was going on before it was too late. He cared a lot and he didn't want to get hurt.

After he left Rocket looked at the information he had in front of him. He advised Poetry Lady not to handle this case. He knew she wouldn't go for it. She just rolled those beautiful eyes.

They would both find out all they could about Mary Trevante. She was a retired school teacher who had her pension and a few dollars saved. She was a very happy lady with nothing stopping her from going away when she had to. This was the only information her father gave them. Not having a social security number made it tough but they would try without it.

Rocket immediately called Dave. He wanted to know if the name was on the FBI computer. You couldn't be too safe these days. Poetry googled her name. In modern times google searches gave you all you needed to know.

Poetry found there were many people by that name. One of them was a mystery writer. She was the one who was closest in age to what her father told them. She led an average life. She wrote twelve books and they all were sellers. Finally, she found a picture of the woman. Her dad didn't have one.

When she left work that day she called her father to meet her at home. She showed him the picture and he said it wasn't her. Poetry promised she would continue looking for her.

Rocket had gone to see Dave to see what he turned up. He was glad that his father-in-law was there. He told him that he did turn up something that disturbed him. Mary had been married three times. Poetry said there was nothing wrong with that. Rocket said that all three of the men died and left big estates. Poetry's father shook his head. This was impossible. He knew nothing about it. Poetry just looked at him and reminded him of Black Widow's. They killed their prey.

Rocket Man warned him about approaching her. He was better off pretending that he knew nothing. The difference in this case was that he had nothing to give her. He wasn't rich. Both Rocket and Poetry told him that they would continue investigating.

Poetry's mother knew that her father was dating. She seemed jealous but by now they hardly spoke to each other. She wasn't dating at all. She really did not like having to check in with any man. She had lunch with Poetry on a Tuesday. Rocket was busy and mother daughter time seemed to be a good thing. They met at Poetry's favorite Italian restaurant, Le Bistro.

Her mother looked good. She took great care of herself. There was a lot of small talk and of course she wanted to know about her grandchildren. Lunch lasted a while and during that time Rocket Man called her. He had new information about Mary. Poetry told him she would be back at the office in twenty minutes. Lunch was almost over.

Chapter Twelve
About Mary Trevante

Rocket was at the office waiting for Poetry Lady. When she got there she saw Dave. Dave didn't look happy. They slowly but surely explained to Poetry Lady what they learned. Mary was indeed a Black Widow. She set up her prey, married them and eventually killed them for money. The fact that Poetry's father didn't have money made no sense at all. She said that to both Dave and Rocket and they told her she was wrong. Her father had been investing in the Stock Market and he had a big hit. He was wealthy. What bothered Poetry the most was that he didn't bother to tell her. She was furious with him again. Now she could see why he was a victim. Rocket had invited Poetry's father to the office and after he calmly sat down he told him what he had told Poetry. Mary had set him up and he had to be prepared for the fact that she could kill him.

Her father laughed and laughed. This was the most ridiculous thing he ever heard. Anyway it didn't matter. He had stopped seeing her a week before. She was going to Europe for several months and he saw that their relationship was going nowhere. Poetry was proud of him that he ended it.

Six months later they read an article in the LA Times. Mary's current husband died in a suspicious boat accident. That could have been her father.

At least that part of his life was over. Rocket smiled when Poetry said that it was difficult raising parents but he knew his kids would someday say that about him.

Chapter Thirteen
Surprise, Surprise

Both Rocket Man & Poetry Lady were glad that things were now calm. He looked at her with such love. They were excited that Ryan was coming home for the holidays. Holidays meant a lot to them. Thanksgiving was a time of love and peace. Ryan was coming home by plane.

Rocket went to the airport with Poetry. The plane was landing at 10 p.m. When they announced the plane the excitement mounted. It took a while for the passengers to come down.

When Poetry saw him she ran to him. He hugged her. He missed his parents. He then turned around and hugged Rocket Man. There was a pretty young girl standing on the side. It was at that moment that Ryan introduced Melissa. He decided to bring her home for Thanksgiving.

Both Rocket and Poetry stared at each other. Why hadn't Ryan asked for permission to bring a friend home?
Who was this friend?
Tune in to the next episode of Rocket Man & Poetry Lady....